MARVEL

AVENGERS ASSEMBLY

ORIENTATION

By Preeti Chhibber

Illustrated by James Lancett

Scholastic Inc.

ISBN 978-1-338-71601-6

1 2020

Printed in the U.S.A.   23
First printing 2020

Book design by Katie Fitch

HERO CARD #148

MS. MARVEL

POWERS

NAME:
KAMALA KHAN, AKA
MS. MARVEL

POWERS:
Embiggening!
Disembiggening!
Stretching!
Shape-shifting!

MARVEL

HERO CARD #477

SPIDER-MAN

POWERS

NAME:
MILES MORALES, AKA
ULTIMATE SPIDER-MAN

POWERS:
Wall-crawling, expo-
nential strength, electric
shocks, being invisible,
but not being creepy like
a spider, that is for sure.

MARVEL

HERO CARD #091

SQUIRREL GIRL
AND TIPPY-TOE

POWERS

NAME:
DOREEN GREEN, AKA SQUIRREL GIRL

POWERS:
Powers of a squirrel and (more importantly) powers of a girl. Prehensile tail! Super good at jumping! A+ empathy!

MARVEL

HERO CARD #065

LOCKJAW

POWERS

NAME:
LOCKJAW

POWERS:
Appearing out of nowhere and scaring the junk out of the people he is with.

MARVEL

CHAPTER 1

At home in Jersey City, Kamala Khan unwinds in her private blog . . .

O O O | EmbiggenFeels.moomblr.private.com

Ups and Ups of that Super Hero Life

Yesterday was **great!**

Beat out a super villain? ☑

EARLIER THAT EVENING . . .

Tinkerer, what do you want?!

For my toys to be sold in all the Jersey City corner stores!!!! I seek . . . DISTRIBUTION!!!

I have to be honest. These . . . aren't great, Tinkerer.

BZZT BZZT

HOW DARE—

KA-PUT!

Fair enough.

PRIVATE ENCRYPTED POST

Okay . . . maybe not a super villain, but a bad dude! And I beat him!

And we don't need to discuss what happened on the way home, that was a fluke.

ANYWAY, I started a new fic and it is all ready to get uploaded!!

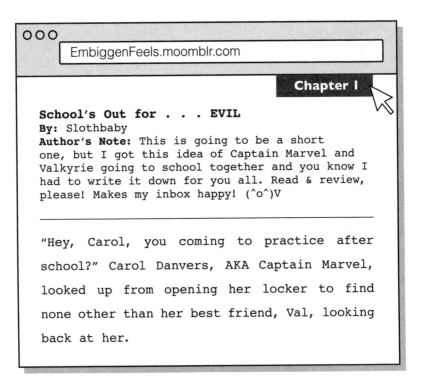

EmbiggenFeels.moomblr.com

Chapter 1

School's Out for . . . EVIL
By: Slothbaby
Author's Note: This is going to be a short one, but I got this idea of Captain Marvel and Valkyrie going to school together and you know I had to write it down for you all. Read & review, please! Makes my inbox happy! (^o^)V

"Hey, Carol, you coming to practice after school?" Carol Danvers, AKA Captain Marvel, looked up from opening her locker to find none other than her best friend, Val, looking back at her.

"Val, uh . . ." How was she going to get out of this? She had secret fight training at S.H.I.E.L.D. after school, but Director Fury had told her no one was allowed to know. "I . . . uh."

Her friend kept looking up at her expectantly.

"What, do you have a HOT DATE or something?" Val waggled her eyebrows, and Carol bit back a laugh.

"Yes! I have a HOT DATE, yep. That's what it is. A hot date. For sure."

She didn't like lying to Val, but Director Fury had said that tonight Carol was going to train with someone really special.

"Well, practice is early because I got places to be, too. So as long as your date's not till later?"

"Ah, right after school, Val. Sorry!" Carol really needed to come up with a reason to quit the basketball team. She couldn't do both! Even if it meant giving up her All-American title; she had another title that meant more.

ON THE OTHER SIDE OF THE HUDSON RIVER, KAMALA HAS A FAN ENJOYING HER LATEST STORY...

Read it out loud! I want to know what happens! *

Okay, okay.*

*Translated from squirrel-ese

"School's Out for EVIL"—dun, dun, dun...

BZZT

The Tinkerer's out of order in Jersey!

...AND IN THE DORMS AT BROOKLYN VISIONS ACADEMY...

Miles! We're gonna be late for study group, dude.

BZZT

Right behind you, Ganke. Just watching this wild video from Jersey!

...

8

JERSEY CITY'S MYSTERIOUS NEW SUPER HERO MS. MARVEL WAS IN TROUBLE EARLIER THIS EVENING. AFTER FACING OFF WITH AND DEFEATING THE TINKERER, MS. MARVEL WAS SHOCKED . . .

BY THE SHOCKER!

THE CITIZENS OF NEW JERSEY WATCHED—AND DODGED—AS THE TWO FOUGHT!

THE SHOCKER PULLED NO PUNCHES, AND JERSEY CITY WAS FEELING IT!

BUT HAVE NO FEAR, JERSEYITES, MS. MARVEL CAME THROUGH.

OVER JUST AS QUICKLY AS IT STARTED, THE BATTLE LEFT NEWARK AVENUE A LITTLE WORSE FOR WEAR. BUT THANKFULLY, OUR NEW HERO GOT THE SHOCKER BACK WHERE HE BELONGS! BEHIND BARS!

BRUNO: Saw the fight with that yellow suited dork today—dang! U gotta watch out, K

KAMALA: ? I did it! I beat him tho?

BRUNO: But the damage ring

KAMALA: It wasn't TOO bad

BRUNO: 👍 but what about next time? Maybe there could be more than one Jersey City super hero? NYC has a gajillion

KAMALA: U think I can't do it?

BRUNO: Help can't hurt?? Y not have a backup for when we're in class?

KAMALA: Ughhhhhh

PRIVATE ENCRYPTED POST

Finally, back into the safety of the best place in the world: my bed.

I can't believe that Bruno thinks I can't be a good super hero on my own. How dare he. It's not like you see Spider-Man trading shifts with someone else! It's so rude. Ugh. UGH.

I've totes got this. I took down two bad guys today all on my own and only broke, like, one part of one building. It's not like anyone got hurt!

That feels like a big win!

I know I can do it. And I know that Bruno's just looking out for me, but it feels pretty blergh that my best friend thinks I'm not good enough to do this stuff on my own. SIGH.

I just have to remember how Captain Marvel does it!

CHAPTER 2

TO: Kamala Khan <k-khan2014@heatmail.com>

FROM: Carol Danvers <cdanvers@avengers-institute.com>

Subject: Welcome to Avengers Institute

Dear Ms. Khan,

Congratulations on your acceptance to Avengers Institute. I am so pleased to offer you a spot at our school.

Busted buildings aside, I was very impressed with your work caught on camera. And I'm here to help you become the hero you're meant to be.

You'll be working alongside other special students being taught by some of the greatest minds the universe has to offer. There is a strict secrecy code at the Institute, so we'll ask you to sign the attached document. For security purposes, we ask that you not discuss your attendance at this school with anyone.

We look forward to seeing what you can accomplish when given the right knowledge and tools. A welcome packet will follow from our acting vice principal, Pietro Maximoff.

Col. Carol Danvers

Principal, Avengers Institute

Kamala's Innermost Thoughts
Hands Off!

CAROL DANVERS KNOWS MY NAME.
Okay. Okay. I have to breathe. It's just the woman who inspired my super hero name, everything is fine.

OMIGODDDDDDDDDD!!!!!

I have to say yes, right? I can't say no to Carol freakin' Danvers! But if I say yes, what am I going to tell Ammi and Abu? And who's going to babysit for my brother's baby? How much time is this going to take?

I guess they technically haven't asked me anything, just told me that I was accepted. Does that mean I have to go?

. . . Wait, Carol knows my name, but it's because she thinks I need to go to some kind of super school? What kind of powered kids have to go to extra training in an after-school program?

WAIT, WAIT, WAIT . . . DOES SHE THINK I'M BAD AT THIS???

Kamala's Innermost Thoughts
Hands Off!

So, I have a lot of thoughts about everything and I'm feeling a little stuck. I don't know if I should go. I'm getting a lot of different answers from people. If it's like that quote from the Quran that Abu always says, "Whoever saves one person it is as if he has saved all of mankind," then I have a responsibility to be the best I can be, right?

I asked Sheik Abdullah (in the most vague way possible) and he said "Kamala, yes, you try as hard as you can. But remember, it is okay to fail. You just try harder the next time." Okay, great, that SORT of makes me feel better. Would he say the same thing if he knew I was IN A PROGRAM FOR SUPER HEROES???

Bruno didn't quite get it. Sure, he knows all about my powers already but he doesn't *really* understand. "A program that Captain freakin' Marvel invited you to? It's going to make you even better than you already are! Kamala, this is gonna be so great! I'm actually jealous . . . !" That's easy for you to say, you're not the one who's gonna have one of the most powerful super heroes in the universe breathing down your neck.

How do you trust new people in your life? I haven't made a new friend since, like, elementary school! Then again, I met Nakia at school when I said I'd make all that food for International Day at school without asking my mom first, like, samosa and paratha and kheer. And I totally ran out of time and it was a distaster? Nakia saved my butt, and we weren't even really friends then! Sometimes you have to trust your instincts on people. Nakia trusted her instincts on me and here we are! I guess I can do that too?

Maybe I need to stop overthinking it?

BruKNOWSBEST:
Maybe u shud do a pros / cons list?

Okay, a pros-and-cons list.

Okay, I can do this.

AVENGERS INSTITUTE

PROS

1 - Captain Marvel invited me and that is literally the best thing that's ever happened to me **in my life.**

2 - There are people there that I could probably actually ask for advice when it comes to super hero stuff because they have real-life experience.

3 - Actually, it will be cool to talk to adults about this stuff without having to talk **around** being a hero!

4 - It's after school so I won't have to figure out how to go to normal high school at the same time.

5 - I bet the classes are going to be really interesting! Omg, I bet there's a class about teleportation. Or going to space! The X-Men are always going to space!

6 - I'LL PROBABLY GET TO MEET AN X-MAN OR MULTIPLE X-MEN. (Sidenote: Is the singular of X-Men X-Man?)

7 - Oh man, I bet Avengers Institute will give me so much fan-fiction inspiration.

8 - Maybe it'll help me figure out how to stay organized even with a side gig. I can't be the only person who accidentally brings her super hero costume to school instead of her gym clothes.

CONS

1 – What if they tell me I shouldn't be a super hero, or that I'm too young, or too inexperienced? What if I disappoint Carol?

2 – What if everyone else is better than me?

3 – Making new friends is **hard**, even if Nakia says it should be easy.

4 – Is it weird to write fanfic about people that I meet IRL?

5 – It's going to be really hard to get all my homework and patrolling done if I'm at this thing every week night. Who's gonna take care of Jersey City? It's not like there are a ton of heroes just hanging out here like there are in New York.

6 – Is the Institute going to give me even more homework???

7 – I'm going to have to come up with a really good excuse for Abu and Ammi to go to this thing every night.

8 – A group of super heroes in one place sounds like an accident waiting to happen . . . I've read a lot of stories about Xavier's school and the Avengers Tower. Someone's always breaking in or targeting them.

9 – Didn't Quicksilver used to be a bad guy???

Great. So helpful. Eight pros and nine cons. Now what?

CHAPTER 3

23

24

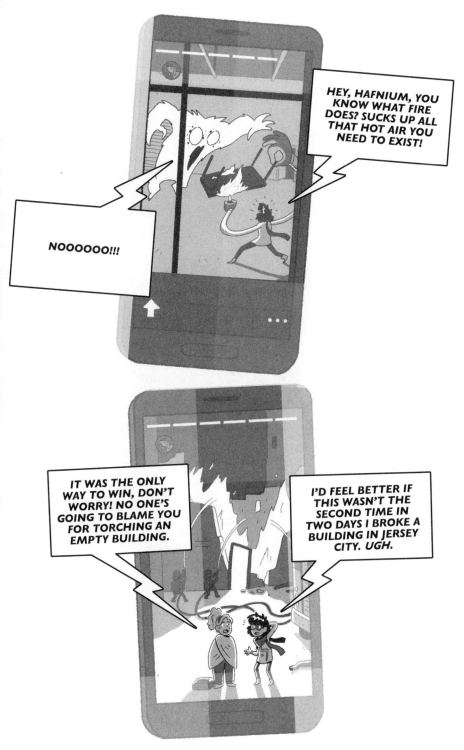

25

PRIVATE ENCRYPTED POST

So, I *did* beat that bully Hafnium, but I accidentally brought a building down in the process. But my friend Mike's safe! So . . . Kamala-2, Universe-1.

Of course, *that's* when . . . Captain Marvel (!!!) and Quicksilver—super-fast and super-good-looking mutant—I mean, Mr. Maximoff—showed up to actually talk to me *In Person* about Avengers Institute. If you're wondering how it went, let me share this brief interaction with you.

Me: *covered in dirt and grime and ash, standing outside a building that I just lit on fire*

Captain Marvel and Quicksilver: *SUDDENLY APPEAR AND LOOK PRISTINE AND PERFECT IN EVERY WAY*

(Literally, I think Mr. Maximoff's hair was actually glinting in the sunshine.)

Me: OMIGOD HELLO HOW ARE YOU HELLO, MA'AM, SIR, HELLO.

Mr. Maximoff: Please, call me Pietro—

Captain Marvel: You can call him Mr. Maximoff, and hello, Ms. Marvel. Nice job taking down Hafnium today. We were watching a video of it on the way in.

Mr. Maximoff: Well, I watched it at home, and then ran over here. Carol needed a bit more time. Not bad, kid.

Me: *throat is too dry to speak, cannot speak*

Captain Marvel and Mr. Maximoff: *wait for me to say something, anything*

The silence lasted way longer than it should have. It was like eight years of no one speaking. It was so awkward.

Captain Marvel: Soooo, have you given any thought to Avengers Institute? We'd love to have you.

So as you can see, it was great. Yeah. Great meeting where I was not completely weird at all and I was totally normal.

Blargh.

Time to update that pros-and-cons list, because added PRO:

• I can go and show Carol that I can speak actual words in sentences.

Especially since I agreed to do it, which is probably a good idea . . . you know, building falling down in a big pile of fire and flames and all. Sigh.

BIG PILE O'ASH

Chapter 2

School's Out for . . . EVIL

By: Slothbaby

"Again!!" Agent Fury took a step back, holstering his dummy laser gun. Carol was floating in the air, sweat shining on her forehead.

"Can we take a quick break, Fury? I need a water."

"Ms. Danvers, do you think that you will be able to break for water during a real battle if aliens are going to descend on New York City?"

Carol sighed in answer.

"That's what I thought. Let's go again. And then I have someone I want you to meet."

"Oh really??" Carol shook the tiredness out of her bones, landing on the training room floor with a soft thump. "Who is it?"

Fury shot her a look she couldn't quite read. Mysterious as ever!

"Later, Captain." For now that nickname just referred to her status on the volleyball team, but one day it'd mean a lot more. Carol pushed up off the ground and into the air again, readying herself for the fight that would get her one step closer to the dream. But before she could start, the high-pitched whine of a door opening distracted her, followed by a familiar voice:

"Oh, sorry, am I early?"

TBC!

Author's note: Can you guess who it is?? Hehehhe, no spoilers, but I think you'll be surprised! I've got some life stuff going on, but trying to get the new chapter up asap!

COMMENTS

W3bbed4Life   Chapter 2 • *5 hours ago*

YO! Slothbaby! This is so good n I can't wait 2 see what happens next!! Is it Val? I hope it's Valkyrie. Also cant wait 2 see who theyre gna fight!

Anonymous   Chapter 2 • *4 hours ago*

Ugghhhh can u plz write Wolverine into this story???? Think he'd be a way better teacher than Fury!

AcornLuvr   Chapter 2 • *2 hours ago*

I LOVE THIS SO MUCH!! UPDATE SOON PLZ <3 <3 <3 <3 I WANNA SEE VALKYRIE AND CAROL HAVE FUN TOGTHER!! CANT WAIT TO READ MORE!!!

Crzy4Cap   Chapter 2 • *1 hour ago*

Hey! This is wonderful, Slothbaby! I have one suggestion, though: maybe one scene with Captain America? I think he'd be a really smart addition to your story!

TO: Kamala Khan <k-khan2014@heatmail.com>

FROM: Pietro Maximoff <pmaximoff@avengers-institute.com>

Subject: Prepping for Avengers Institute

Hello, Ms. Khan,

Please expect a box from Avengers Institute to show up in your room shortly. This will provide you with a bag and some other special items you'll need for your time in school. You'll find the item list attached to this email, please let me know if you're missing anything on the list. I'd hate for a missing piece of tech to end up in . . . the wrong hands. In addition to those, we ask that you bring the following:

- Your costume (and an extra if you have two)
- Notebook
- Writing utensils
- A graphing calculator
- Emergency contact information of someone you trust

You'll also see a blank form attached here. We use it as a little Q&A to send to the teachers to get to know you. Please fill it out and send it back to me before your first day. Lastly, you'll see your course schedule attached.

Best,

Pietro Maximoff
Vice Principal, Avengers Institute

ITEM LIST FOR AVENGERS ASSEMBLY

- One Avengers Institute duffel bag

- One Avengers Institute puffer jacket

- One Avengers Institute planner

- One Avengers Institute combination lock

- One Avengers Institute hologram ID card

- One Avengers Institute standard time & space traveling wristwatch communicator

Oooh. Nice logo.

NAME: Ms. Marvel

NICKNAMES: Double M, Stretch

INTERESTS: Nerd stuff, video games, comics, fan fiction

POWERS: Embiggening and disembiggening, stretching, healing, shape-shifting

WEAKNESSES: Electricity and sometimes needing ALL THE GYROS to refuel.

How do I even answer this?

HOMETOWN: Jersey City, NJ!

PRONOUNS: She/her

CHAPTER 4

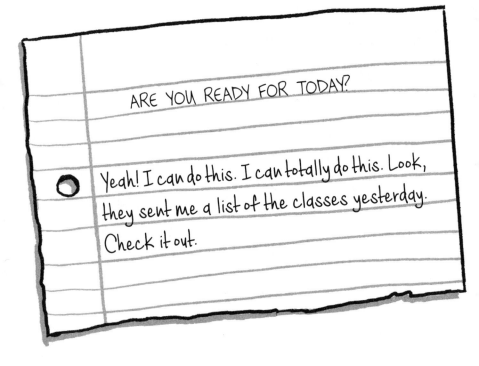

ARE YOU READY FOR TODAY?

Yeah! I can do this. I can totally do this. Look, they sent me a list of the classes yesterday. Check it out.

My Class Schedule

Monday:
INTRODUCTION TO BEING A HERO
with visiting professor Dr. Hank McCoy, AKA BEAST. (This
is the giant blue mutant who says "Oh my stars and garters!"—
whatever that means lol.)

Tuesday:
RIGHTS AND WRONGS AND IN BETWEEN
with Professor Jennifer Walters, Esquire. She's the She-Hulk
and that name is exactly what it sounds like: awesome lady
Hulk who is also a high-powered attorney.

Wednesday:
INTERDIMENSIONAL TRAVEL & DIPLOMACY with
Professors Lockjaw and Crystal. (Don't know these two . . .)

Thursday:
THE MINIATURE WORLD AND YOU
with Professor Scott Lang. This dude is Ant-Man and this is a
smol class for smol heroes.

41

THE OTHER SPIDER-MAN: Okay, remember: Bring an extra clean costume, trust me. Also, if your vice principal asks you to do any favors "off the books" just say no. Trust me.

MILES: Why would he ask me any favors?

THE OTHER SPIDER-MAN: Quicksilver has his moods.

MILES: That sounds really ominous and I don't like it, man.

THE OTHER SPIDER-MAN: It'll be fine!

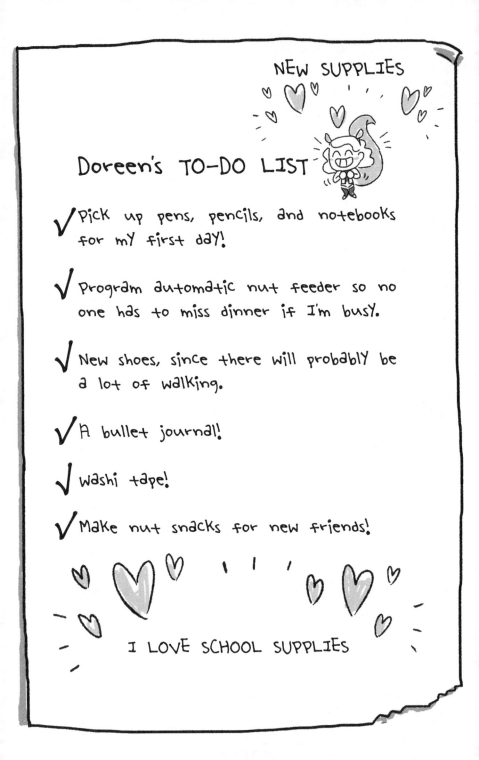

NEW SUPPLIES

Doreen's TO-DO LIST

✓ Pick up pens, pencils, and notebooks for my first day!

✓ Program automatic nut feeder so no one has to miss dinner if I'm busy.

✓ New shoes, since there will probably be a lot of walking.

✓ A bullet journal!

✓ Washi tape!

✓ Make nut snacks for new friends!

I LOVE SCHOOL SUPPLIES

45

Wow! I had no idea there were so many heroes in Jersey!

Oh, we're not in Jersey. There are just a bunch of empty buildings, then Professor Lockjaw goes to pick the new students up.

You'll get an Avengers pass at orientation, and that's how you get to and from the school. It's amazing.

It's actually something about how we get disassembled into particles and then reassembled in our bedrooms, I think? Reed Richards came up with it.

Like, from the Fantastic Four?

ARISE! I HAVE ANIMATED YOU!

Did you hear that?

Today was interesting! We didn't actually start school yet, it was more just a getting-to-learn-the-system day, which was nice. I didn't have to worry about actually having to know stuff yet. Spider-Man and Squirrel Girl are great! We ended up eating a snack together and hero-watching (the super hero version of people watching). Turns out they're both nerds! (And as a nerd, I obviously love nerds.)

I mean, Spidey does seem a little overwhelmed—and Squirrel Girl is all over the place. I'm not sure how well we'd fight bad guys together? I don't even know how we'd organize. Who would make the calls? Whose fault would it be if things go wrong? HOW DO TEAMS WORK?

And, on top of that, everyone else seems so put together! I saw a policeman from outerspace called **Nova** do a barrel flip in the hallway. In real life. Right in front of my eyes. These eyes!

I wonder how everyone else ended up at the Institute. I'll have to ask Spidey and Squirrel Girl when I see them tomorrow. Because . . . you know. Like, who told all these super heroes they had to start an after-hours school?? They're all so . . . cool. Not that being cool is a must for being a hero. Okay, maybe what I mean is that they're all so confident in their abilities. At least, that's what it seems like.

There were some weird kids who, uh, may have dipped into the dark arts. I think one of them may have created a tiny monster. I swear I saw something climb out of the trash can.

But Squirrel Girl said a teacher would handle it. There was a disturbing amount of maniacal laughter, though . . .

CHAPTER 5

STARK

THE OTHER SPIDER-MAN: Kid, did I just get a news alert about Spider-Man dropping a full burrito on an arrest in progress allowing the criminal to use crema to slip out of his cuffs and GET AWAY?

MILES: I was late for class! But I know, I should try not to eat and swing.

THE OTHER SPIDER-MAN: I've been there, and I get it. I do. But you have more options! My friend Carol put together an after-school program that I think would be great for you.

MILES: Did you have to go to an after-school hero school?

THE OTHER SPIDER-MAN: Look, I dropped my breakfast sandwich on J. Jonah Jameson's head two days ago, and while I pretended it was on purpose, it definitely wasn't. I haven't had time to wash my suit in four days. And the Human Torch had to buy me lunch yesterday because I left my wallet in one of the X-Jets (don't ask). I *wish* there had been after-school hero school when I was growing up.

MILES: 😆

THE OTHER SPIDER-MAN: I think this thing will help you get a handle on how all the parts of your life fit together. School, family, work, super heroing.

MILES: Okay. I'm sorry about the burrito.

THE OTHER SPIDER-MAN: It's okay— happens to everyone. Except maybe Captain America. But let's make a pact to not eat and swing unless it's an emergency. 🤝

MILES: Deal . . . Dollar slices count as an emergency, right?

THE OTHER SPIDER-MAN: 🍕 + 😋 = 👍

SQUIRREL GIRL
GETS LIFETIME PASS

NEW YORK, NEW YORK—Local hero Squirrel Girl recently saved thousands of people at a theme park in upstate New York, and in doing so, got herself a lifetime pass to enjoy the fun-time rides for as long as she wants to. When asked for comment, Squirrel Girl had this say: "I'm going to ride the Emu's Flight five times *in a row*—Chuuuuuk chuk chuk chuk chuuuuuk chuk—wait, are there no animals allowed? Tippy-Toe wants to know the park's rules about squirrel height."

SQUIRREL GIRL SAVES THRILL SEEKERS

ALBANY, NEW YORK—
Theme park–goers in LAKE
HAROLD, NEW YORK,
were shocked when bolts of
manmade lightning struck
every ride at once, stalling
some visitors as high as
four hundred feet. Luck-
ily, Squirrel Girl was in the
area to bring a horde of her
bushy-tailed friends and
save the day by swooping in

THE TEAMS

Team 1:
MOON GIRL & DEVIL DINOSAUR

Okay, this team is a nine-year-old girl genius from the Lower East Side with her pet dinosaur. Yep.

Team 2:
AMERICA CHAVEZ, WASP (NADIA VAN DYNE), NOVA

Awesomely strong girl who can travel between dimensions, the new Wasp (AKA the original Ant-Man's kid), and a space super hero policeman.

Team 3:
MAX FRANKENSTEIN,
KID IMMORTUS,
DEATH LOCKET,
KID APOCALYPSE

Prince of Bavaria, and last descendant of Victor Von Frankenstein; X-Men super bad guy and oldest mutant ever; time-traveling kid from the 30th century (maybe related to Dr. Doom?); synthetic cyborg girl, and young clone of Apocalypse.

Team 4:
PATRIOT, AMADEUS CHO, IRONHEART

New York City's newest young Super-Soldier, Korean-American Genius (AKA Brawn), and an amazing girl from Chicago who made her own Iron Man suit. Wow.

Team 5:

SPIDER-MAN, MS. MARVEL, SQUIRREL GIRL!

Us. Team 5. Brooklyn Spider-Man, our rodent-powered friend, and me.

PRIVATE ENCRYPTED POST

SUBJECT: EX-SQUEEZE ME?

F(Finding)out that we have an ACADEMIC DECATH-
LON AT THE END OF THE SEMESTER IN WHICH WE
ARE GOING TO COMPETE AGAINST EACH OTHER OR
SOMETHING?:

Why is this A Thing? Why can't we all just
agree that everyone learned a lot and we're
all great, The End?

y tho

SM & SG told me that
it would probably be
fine. It'll be fine.
We're all fine here.
Everything's great.

Basically, it went like this:

Me: So the classes all sound pretty cool, but, like . . . are they grading us? Do we get report cards?

Me, but from the future: YOU ARE GONNA WISH IT WAS REPORT CARDS.

SG: WE'RE GOING TO GET TO COMPETE IN AN ACADEMIC DECATHLON.

SM: What SG also meant to say is that it's with teams so it'll be okay. My mentor always says that team-ups are totally worth the hassle . . . Not sure why he used the word "hassle" but he sounded positive! Mostly.

SG: We should be on a team together!

Me: So . . . All your base are belong to us basically?

And that's how I ended up on an academic decathlon team in an after-school program so BRB while I do an internet search for "how to not be stressed."

P.S. SM laughed at my riff on a retro game joke, so . . . maybe I'm making friends?

Comment on EX-SQUEEZE ME? from BruKNOWIT

waits patiently for you to come home and tell me who SM and SG are

There was another weird (small! But weird) thing that happened today . . .

So, that was strange. Why was Kid Apocalypse staring at us? I'm pretty sure he was also with the weird, shady kids from earlier.

He looked worried, which makes me worried.

You know, all these feelings have me almost looking forward to just sitting in science class tomorrow. At least there I know how to act, and who my friends are, and where the cafeteria is. And how to get into my locker.

. . . Also, I know the vice principal isn't going to call me into the office to listen to bizarro advice!

ADVICE FROM VICE PRINCIPAL MAXIMOFF

*With notes from his student, Ms. Marvel

1. *Always* be aware of your surroundings.

See what I was saying about making me nervous?

2. Don't fall in love with a robot.

?????

3. Running away always seems like an attractive option, but use it as a last resort.

Okay, I can understand this one coming from a super-speedy hero.

4. Addendum to the above: unless you can run away really fast and get help.

This seems . . . really specific to like two other heroes.

5. Give everyone a chance to change, you might be surprised.

CHAPTER 6

First week of classes! We're kicking off with Professor McCoy's beginner's class. I can't believe I'm taking a class where BEAST is the teacher. He is iconic, literally! I heard a rumor that the X-Men use his face as their Wiki-icon on their phones!

Phone icon!

INTRODUCTION TO BEING A HERO

What is a hero?
Maybe start the class by asking students to define?

PROFESSOR: Visiting Professor Henry McCoy

OVERVIEW: A beginning course for powered peoples new to the super hero life.

OBJECTIVE: Prepare young heroes for the world by sharing our histories, teaching teamwork skills, and practical application of various powers.

NOTES:

- Pay attention to stories teachers tell and learn through our mistakes and our successes.

- ABCs of working on a team:

  o Active Listening

  o Be Assertive

  o Creative Solutions

- The common criminals and how to defeat them safely.

- How to work together with our non-powered friends to protect our communities.

Yesterday's class was a doozy. I think Professor McCoy's lucky that his blue fur covers his cheeks so we couldn't see if he was blushing LOL. Today we've got our first class with She-Hulk, and I am very nervous to meet her. She's only starred in . . . three of my fanfics??

I have to be cool. I can be cool. "Kamala Khan: She's cool." That's what kids say about me. Yup.

I'm a little nervous about what lives in between rights and wrongs because what does that even mean?

FILE NAME: RIGHTS AND WRONGS AND IN BETWEEN
PROFESSOR JENNIFER WALTERS, ESQUIRE

PROCEDURAL HISTORY: Students have been invited to attend
AVENGERS INSTITUTE for a variety of reasons including, but
not limited to, failed villain apprehension, accidental building
demolition, tendencies to toe the line of lawful and lawless. Et
cetera.

ISSUE: How do we define right and wrong? What does it mean
to be good? To do good?

A TRANSCRIPT OF OPENING REMARKS

JENNIFER WALTERS, ESQUIRE, AKA SHE-HULK: Hello,
class, I'm Professor Walters—

DOREEN GREEN, AKA SQUIRREL GIRL: Professor Walters, I
am such a fan I have all your action cards and I've read every
fanfic about you on FanFic Haven.

KAMALA KHAN, AKA MS. MARVEL: Omigod, you're on
FanFic Haven? I'm on Moomblr!!!

MILES MORALES, AKA SPIDER-MAN: Me too!

SHE-HULK: Let's table the fan fiction! Although, maybe at
some point we can talk about how if you're going to write a
story that I'm in, to please remember that I have a law degree.
They always leave that out in my fan fiction . . .

MS. MARVEL, MUMBLING: Note to self: Go back and make
sure all my old fics mention that law degree.

SHE-HULK: Now, as I was saying—and thank you for the kind words, Squirrel Girl—but, I want to talk to you about right and wrong.

BARON MAXIMILIAN VON KATZENELNBOGEN, AKA MAX FRANKENSTEIN: That's easy! Right is whatever gets you to the goal.

SHE-HULK: Well, that's an interesting way of looking at it. What if you win, but you hurt someone innocent? Does that still feel right?

MS. MARVEL: No . . . because if you're willing to hurt innocent people, then how are you different from the bad guy?

SHE-HULK: These are the questions I want you to ask yourselves! Over the next few weeks, I'm going to bring in some guest lecturers, we're going to look at case studies, and do some experiments. It's going to be fun!

LET THE RECORD SHOW THAT THE CLASS GROANED IN RESPONSE. EXCEPT DOREEN.

SQUIRREL GIRL: OMG YAY!

I should have answered Professor Walters's question yesterday about what is good because I know that we do good.

But then I guess the question is what does good mean in that statement?

My head hurts.

ANYWAY, today is the class I've been most excited about!

Interdimensional Travel & Diplomacy—we're going to travel to another dimension!!!! The diplomacy part's probably going to be pretty easy. I mean, I know how to talk to aunties, and they're a tough crowd. Politicians don't have anything on aunties.

So places I'm guessing we're going:

Another planet, probably. I feel like super heroes are always hanging out in space.

Ooh, I have to remember to get Bruno some postcards for his collection!

Greetings from MARS

Hey, Bruno!

GUESS WHERE THIS POST CARD IS FROM? MARS! There is a gift shop on MARS. I can't believe in our first Interdimensional Travel class they took us to M-A-R-S.

I'll keep picking these things up for you wherever I can since I know you still have that postcard collection. Even though you pretend you don't. Embrace your inner dork!

. . . Now to figure out how to mail this thing . . .

Beep blorp blurp,

-K

NEW ATTILAN

BRUNO,

New Attilan is very cool. I picked up some Attilanian chits (that's their money) and think we should totally start a currency collection (just saying).

So my teachers are Professors Lockjaw and Crystal and it turns out that Professor Crystal is Vice Principal Maximoff's ex-wife. Bruno, I think I'm in a soap opera. And none of my new friends are in

this class to talk about it! Just that weird kid I told you about, the one who keeps staring?

They are definitely teaching us diplomacy, though. I just learned how to greet Inhuman royalty. I'll show you at school tomorrow!

-K

B-Car! (Just trying to jazz up these greetings.)

So, we are on Knowhere and inside of a head and I think that's making my head hurt? I think the point of this visit was for our teachers to show us that diplomacy doesn't always work. And I'm definitely spelling that alien name wrong, but Professor Crystal was screaming it while we were running, so I can't be sure on the exact transcription

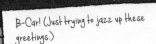

there. Oh, but that weird kid? Turns out he's just super shy. His name's Kid Apocalypse (yikes), but he's actually not that bad!

-K

I love the Negative Zone

Bruno,

Just call me negative Nancy. I mean don't, but we're in the Negative Zone.

It's, um, pretty scary. But Professor Lockjaw is the best giant dog to be around, his presence is so comforting. That said, holy cats! The Negative Zone is wild. I think I found a machine from back when the Fantastic Four mapped this whole thing out. It just kept repeating "Johnny, no!" which is . . . dramatic

and just a tiny bit uncomfortable to hear.

Evan and I were not into it.

Hopefully, next time they take us somewhere sparkly and full of rainbows.

See you later!

-K

TO: Kamala Khan <k-khan2014@heatmail.com>

FROM: Carol Danvers <cdanvers@avengers-institute.com>

SUBJECT: INDEPENDENT STUDY

Ms. Khan,

I'm pleased to share that you'll be able to attend an independent study this semester. The classes will alternate week to week. Your first week will be with Scott Lang, AKA Ant-Man. Since you're the only attendee with size powers, you'll be the sole student in Professor Lang's class: The Miniature World and You. Despite the name, I believe that he'll also discuss how to engage when you increase your size.

Professor Lang just liked the sound of the class name. Please don't ask him why he won't change it.

As always, you're welcome to email me with any questions you might have.

Best,

Col. Carol Danvers
Principal, Avengers Institute

Liked by STARS&GARTERS, CassLang10, and 4 others

SLANG181 This is what you call being a TEACHER. I risk it all for my precious student!

QuickAG Professor Lang, is one student too much for you?

SLANG181 @QuickAG No sir! This was all part of the plan.

Liked by STARS&GARTERS, QuickAG, and 15 others

SLANG181 And that's how you save someone. Boom! Taught!

CarolDanvers Scott, let's chat tomorrow.

SLANG181 Yes @CarolDanvers

CHAPTER 7

MEANWHILE, IN THE ONLY SECRET LAIR THEY CAN PULL TOGETHER IN THIS SUPER HERO SCHOOL, WE FIND A GROUP OF COLLEAGUES-OF-CONVENIENCE: KID IMMORTUS, DEATH LOCKET, MAX FRANKENSTEIN, AND KID APOCALYPSE. AKA THEY'RE KINDA BAD. THIS IS NOT GOING TO END WELL.

I need to make it back to the timestream*! The future is crying out for me.

This century is absurd. They don't even have affordable teleportation. Accessible tele-portation should be a fundamental right!

If I could just find out the next time Thor is in town . . .

All that's missing in my equation is the lightning. Just the lightning for REANIMATION!

Do . . . you think this thing streams WebFlix?

*THIS IS TIME . . . BUT LIKE, A SUPERHIGHWAY VERSION OF TIME.

HERO CARD #213

DEATH LOCKET

POWERS

MARVEL

NAME:
DEATH LOCKET

KNOWN ALIASES:
Rebecca, Becca

POWERS:
Stretching,
super strength,
indestructible, healing
factor, part robot

WEAKNESSES:
Yeah, right

HERO CARD

#813

KID IMMORTUS

POWERS

NAME:
KID IMMORTUS

KNOWN ALIASES:
Nathan

POWERS:
Tactician, super intellect, born leader, can time travel *without* throwing up

WEAKNESSES:
Throwing up

GETTING BACK INTO THE TIMESTREAM BRAINSTORM NOTES

By Kid Immortus

- Escape from this school and hunt down Victor Von Doom and steal his time machine.
  - o Pros: The time machine is ready-made.
  - o Cons: Much as I hate to admit it, Doom would be a formidable enemy.
- Find and excavate the tomb of the pharaoh Rama-Tut—rumor is there's an amulet that would help my cause.
  - o Pros: No extra villains to beat.
  - o Cons: I'm not an archaeologist. What tools do they even use?
- Convince Vice Principal Maximoff to run as fast as he can around the world against its rotation thereby opening a hole in time as the Earth's rotation slows. Maybe. I saw it in a movie and it looked like it could work.
  - o Pros: VP Maximoff seems anxious sitting in his office. Would probably be pretty easy to get him on board.
  - o Cons: Unclear if it would actually work. Would need to do a significant amount of research and preparation.
- Spy on the other students here and see if I can harness their power to get me to the timestream.
  - o Pros: I don't have to escape or sneak or talk to an adult. Just watch.
  - o Cons: Won't know until I see if there's someone to use!

HERO CARD #911

MAX FRANKENSTEIN

POWERS

NAME:
MAXIMILIAN
FRANKENSTEIN

KNOWN ALIASES:
Max, Baron Maximilian
von Katzenelnbogen

POWERS:
High intelligence, some
may say "genius"—a
master of the biological
arts

WEAKNESSES:
N/A

MARVEL

HERO CARD #611

KID APOCALYPSE

POWERS

NAME:
KID APOCALYPSE

KNOWN ALIASES:
Evan Sabahnur

POWERS:
Super strong, healing
factor, shape-shifting,
energy blasts

WEAKNESSES:
Confidence (Lack of)

MARVEL

date:

Doctor's Log,

I am back on this wretched journey. The monster hunts me ever farther. I must find a way to stall it! Through tricks and trade I've managed to come into possession of all the parts I need for a new creation. A creation that will save my skin! A creation that will fight off that thing made by my many times over great-grandfather.

All that's missing is knowing the precise moment lightning will strike, giving me the power I need to create my own Monster.

But how can I predict lightning?

Perhaps the puzzle is not in prediction but in predetermination! I shall make my own energy source. My own bolt. Who am I if not the master of my own destiny?

Evan's Journal KEEP OUT

I thought this school was going to be a way to help me figure things out, to find out where I'm supposed to be.

I guess this is it? With a crew of kids mad at the world. It fits, though. Kid Immortus is the leader (though sometimes Max has a thing or two to say about that). And I'm Kid Apocalypse. Maybe it's fate.

I wish, sometimes, that I could just be Evan.

Guess that just isn't in my future. And that makes me wonder about what is in my future.

. . . Anyway, other than that the school is fine. The classes are interesting. I really like the one with Professor Lockjaw and Professor Crystal. None of my friends are in it, but we get to go everywhere! And Ms. Marvel's in that class with me. She's been nice. I think we're becoming friends, which is cool. (I'm trying to be not-weird about this, but I am really excited!)

Chapter 3

School's Out for . . . EVIL

By: Slothbaby

"Sorry, am I early?"

Carol's head snaps back at the voice, excitement already visible on her face.

"MONICA!!" Her best friend in the whole entire world just walked into her training station. Monica Rambeau. Carol flew over to her and threw her arms around Monica. "WHEN DID YOU GET HERE?"

"Carol!" Monica laughed, returning the hug. "Just got in a few minutes ago, and they said you were already here!"

Monica was training in a similar program to Carol's, only she was going to be a pilot. So she flew around the world with her teachers. Carol was only a tiny bit jealous.

"What are you doing tonight? I've been waiting for you to get home so we can watch the new season of—"

"Ahem."

"Oh, sorry, sir."

"Ms. Rambeau, you are welcome to join Ms. Danvers in her training, but otherwise, I'll recommend that you watch from the sidelines."

Monica had gone into salute mode at Fury's interruption.

"Yes, sir." But her lip twitched as she looked at Carol, promises of a future hang-out session in her eyes.

"Okay, Captain, let's see how you handle these lasers." Fury turned back to Carol and laughed in that way that always made her nervous.

Carol groaned and bent her knees, preparing to launch into the air and dodge some friggin' lasers.

ZOOM

She felt the buzz of electricity, and all the hair on her arm rose up as a laser barely missed her.

"Whoa, cutting it a little close there, sir! Usually, you tell me we're starting!"

"DANVERS, THAT WASN'T OURS, WATCH OUT—" Fury's voice sounded far away, Carol looked down and found him struggling against a masked man.

Then an explosion rocked the ship. Uh-oh.

A/N: Can you tell I love cliffhangers? Mwha ha ha ha.

PRIVATE MESSAGES

 W3bbed4Life   TO: Slothbaby • 7 hours ago

Just private messaging to say:
MONICA!! YES!!!!!! MONIIICCAAAA!! Srsly loving
how this story is going!

 Slothbaby   TO: W3bbed4Life • 6 hours ago

wait, is this . . . DO YOU GO TO A SPECIAL
PROGRAM FOR UH GIFTED KIDS BC I THINK WE KNOW
EACH OTHER I R L

 W3bbed4Life   TO: Slothbaby • 5 hours ago

Yooooo, yes, yes, I think we do. Did we talk
about this in LEGALESE?

 Slothbaby   TO: W3bbed4Life • 4 hours ago

YES, SPIDEY, WHAT UP?

 W3bbed4Life   TO: Slothbaby, AcornLuvr • 4 hours ago

I gotta add Squirrel Girl to this.

 AcornLuvr   TO: Slothbaby, W3bbed4Life • 3 hours ago

HEY, FRIENDS! IT'S ME! SQUIRREL GIRL!

 Slothbaby   TO: AcornLuvr, W3bbed4Life • 1 hour ago

z0mgz0mgz0mgz0mg

CHAPTER 8

89

91

Well, that went well. WELL. Well. WELLLLL.
It did not go well.

Professor McCoy was so disappointed. (And who can blame him? Not me.)

So Professor McCoy put us in a room, and we were supposed to team up with our decathlon teams. Me, Spider-Man, and Squirrel Girl. But, everything just happened really fast? Jersey City has never been run over by tiny, creepy, crawling alien things. At least, not while I've been protecting it.

That girl, Death Locket, looked like she was having fun. And I don't think that Max Frankenstein even noticed what was going on, but the rest of us?

At least we weren't the only team that messed up. Ugh, and poor Evan. He's been having trouble controlling his energy blasts.

Like this journal entry, the whole thing was all over the place! I just knew that if I could embiggen, those things couldn't stop me. But I guess I should have talked to my teammates.

But evil rat alien things!!

But also my team. Argh!
Would I have been okay if I'd been on my own?

Professor McCoy was not happy.

Advice from Dr. McCoy:

- Develop a "shorthand" so we can make fast decisions as a team.
  - But what does that mean? I say "Spider-Man, Squirrel Girl! Blorp!" and they'll know I mean: "Spider-Man, I'll embiggen and take the right flank so that you can swing to the left flank from my arm, and then Squirrel Girl will go up the middle with her super strength and squirrel minions!"
- Do trust exercises.
  - I trust Spider-Man and Squirrel Girl, but . . . I've never seen them in action. I don't know what they fight like or how they—oh. Maybe I need to get to know my team better.
- Appoint roles—who is the leader, who handles backup, who makes sure that everyone knows what's going on?
  - Do I just say YES, HI, HELLO. I AM THE LEADER NOW. How does a democracy work with three people? Is this not a super hero-ocracy? Is this a super hero-tator-ship?
- Figure out the best way for all your powers to work together.
  - There has to be a way to do this—come on, Kamala! You've got this.

NO, NO, TALKING TO MYSELF IN THE THIRD PERSON IS TOO WEIRD AND IT IS NOT FOR ME.

Okay, I've got this! I can do it! I hope. Oh gosh. Can I?

Hey, team! Trying out this wrist-watch thing. So, two things: You both are totally reading my Captain Marvel fanfic and it's great! But also never read it in front of me. Second: I think we need to have a hang-out session that's getting to know each other? So we can do all the things Professor McCoy talked about. What do you think?

Ms. M. These are cool. Whoa. Look at my face. I really need to know when Val's going to show back up in School's Out for Evil. And yeah, agreed. He did say we should pick roles, so I nominate you for leader.

Seconding that nomination and it passes!

96

BRUNO: They made u leader? That's awesome n a little scary.

KAMALA: Tell me about it. It all happened vry quickly.

BRUNO: Not 2 pile on but Nakia says she texted u about ur group project and u didn't answer.

KAMALA: #HeadDesk

BRUNO: said I'd mention it sryyyyy

KAMALA: nah it's good thx, I think Spider-Man has a reminder app. Gotta ask him about it.

BRUNO: Oh SPIDER-MAN has one? Do u know Spider-Man? U hadn't mentioned.

KAMALA: omg stahp

BRUNO: lol

CHAPTER 9

The setting: KHAN FAMILY HOME. KITCHEN.
ALMOST DINNER TIME.

The players: MUNEEBA KHAN (AKA MOM), NAKIA, KAMALA
KHAN, AAMIR KHAN (AKA BIG BROTHER)

SCENE I

NAKIA and KAMALA are sitting at the table doing homework.
MUNEEBA is cooking dinner. There are cannisters of spices
littering the countertops. Two pots sit simmering on the stove.
MUNEEBA is rolling out a thin piece of dough. AAMIR is
standing in front of the open fridge, staring.

MUNEEBA: Will you be staying for dinner, Nakia? I can make a
few extra chapati for you.

NAKIA: [looking up from her notebook] You know I can't say no
to your chapati, Auntie!

KAMALA: [rolling her eyes] Mom, my friends will always stay
for dinner.

MUNEEBA: Only asking, beta. Next time you'll say I'm not
polite. [also rolling her eyes, like mother, like daughter]

AAMIR: When is Abu getting home? I need to ask him about
something.

KAMALA: What's that?

AAMIR: None of your business!

MUNEEBA: [flipping a chapati on the pan like only a South Asian mom can, utensil free and using her fingers] Kamala, tell me about these after-school study sessions and clubs. How are they going?

KAMALA: [frantically looking around] Uhhhh.

NAKIA: [being a very good friend, steps in] They're going great, Mrs. Khan! I go to the one on Tuesdays—

MUNEEBA: I thought you went on Thursdays?

NAKIA: RIGHT! Yes, Thursdays. Ha ha. Sorry. What was I thinking? I must have gotten up too early today. Not enough sleep.

KAMALA: [kicking NAKIA under the table]

MUNEEBA: [turning around, holding a ladle covered in daal] This is such an Amreekan problem. None of you children sleep enough. Always working. Look at these dark circles under Kamala's eyes.

KAMALA: Ammi!!

AAMIR: [looking as holier-than-thou as he can] See, Kamala, you should sleep more so you can have a smooth, well-rested face like mine.

KAMALA: [puts her head down on the table and groans]

NAKIA: Kamala, maybe we should finish this project up upstairs.

SCENE II

THE SETTING: KAMALA'S BEDROOM

NAKIA: So what's this after-school program I'm apparently going to with you?

KAMALA: It's a . . . [Kamala pauses and looks around like people are listening in, even though they're alone] super hero school thing.

NAKIA: Ooooh. A super hero SCHOOL?

KAMALA: I know. Captain Marvel thinks I need to go to school to be better. And that I should be on a team. Which—my teammates are great! I do like them, but . . . I don't know, we just had a really bad team-up. Then they made me the leader! I have to trust these people with my life. And it's scary. Which is not a thing a super hero is supposed to feel!

NAKIA: First of all: Everyone gets scared. I bet even Captain Marvel has been scared. And so you had a bad team-up—that's what practice is for! School's there so that we can get smarter, so a super hero school should be there . . . so you can get better at heroing . . . right? And why not a team?

KAMALA: It seems like I should already know how to do this on my own, and adding other people in is hard. Plus, I don't think this school existed for all those grown-up heroes, and they're doing okay.

NAKIA: Okay isn't great, though, Kamala. This school, and having a team that can cover your back—that's a good thing. Trusting people is scary for sure, but think about the possibilities if you do. That could make you great.

KAMALA: Well, that does sound good. I mean, great!

NAKIA: Now, about me covering for you . . .

KAMALA: Nakia totally covered for me n that is a tru friend. Course, then she said that to thank her I couldn't skip out on Sheikh Abdullah's youth lecture @ the mosque

BRUNO: What's the subject this week?

KAMALA: In a hilarious twist of fate, it's about connecting and building bridges and u know, the stuff that im stressed about

BRUNO: sounds like a win-win!

KAMALA: or the universe laughing

BRUNO: or the universe *providing*

KAMALA: lol k good point

BRUNO: speaking of the universe, got any big trips planned in that next travel course?

KAMALA: don't know yet!—oh but you know that kid evan? The one who's cloned from the worst Apocalypse, AKA scariest mutant ever?

BRUNO: oh yeah rough stuff, have u talked to him?

KAMALA: not rly, was thinking of seeing if he'd join our team

BRUNO: y not? You said he's cool, right

KAMALA: Yeah, in the travel class he's great— but in the other classes with his friends, he's super quiet and weird

BRUNO: maybe he needs someone to be a good friend?

KAMALA: that's what I was thinking!

Nakia said something to me about trusting my teammates. And I think that's what I was really afraid of doing. So, I ~~thought that~~ . . . I should tell them who I am. I told Bruno and Nakia about being Ms. Marvel because I needed to. I mean, I have known them my whole life and only known Spider-Man and Squirrel Girl a short while, ~~but~~ I really need to get it together. Okay, this is a good plan. This is a leader's plan. This is how you build a team! Right?

I hope so. Because I am going to see if Squirrel Girl and Spider-Man really want to go all in on this team and share our real faces. Ah!! Gotta do it like ripping off a Band-Aid. BRB.

Hey, buds! I have an . . . idea as, uh, team leader. I think that we should tell each other our real identities. That might help us trust one another. I don't know about you, but trusting new friends is kind of scary.

Well . . . They told us to be careful about sharing our secrets, but don't they also want us to be on a team? A bit confusing don't you think . . .

I won't lie, makes me a little nervous. One of the first things they teach us is to protect the face!

But think about how good we'll be as a team, Spidey!! Count of three? One . . .

I'm Kamala! Nice to meet you both . . . uh.

No you're right. Two . . .

I'm Miles, and same. This is good. I can feel it.

Three!

Okay, I don't have a mask, but my real name is Doreen Green!

And then it was fine. They're just two normal kids like me! We talked about being super heroes and having to do that and go to TWO schools. And homework! Miles and I are both taking the same math level, so after training next week, we're going to have a study session. I have super hero friends omg omg omg.

I'm still nervous about it, I mean, this is a Big Deal. But I really do think it'll make us better at what we do. Just knowing who my teammates really are already makes me feel like we're closer. We'll see how training goes!

$$\underline{x = mc^2}$$

NEW "KID IMMORTUS GETS BACK TO THE TIMESTREAM" PLAN (by me, kid Immortus):

$$\phi = \int \vec{B} \cdot dA$$

$z = x$

I've now done some reconnaissance on Ms. Marvel. She can grow and shrink and stretch. That got me thinking: What part of her is stretching? Is it that her skin is extra stretchy? But she can also shape-shift? How does that even make sense!!

I'll tell you how. I believe she is just in a constant state of time travel. What does time travel have to do with stretchy skin, kid Immortus?

IT'S IN THE MOLECULES!! Those teeny-tiny bits that make her up. They go back and forth in time. Each one a tiny little time machine. It's the only way. I mean, just look at the math.

I am a GENIUS.

I'll share my findings with the group, but I truly believe I've cracked the code!

$-\Omega$

$\cancel{\vec{B} = \vec{w} \times x}$

$w = w^2 + \alpha \cdot t$

A

α

B

$???$

Doctor's Log, date: **censored**

    I've hacked this school's ridiculous matter movers: These wristwatches they provided. Ha! So simple, a child could have done it. (And, you know, one did.) Now all that remains is for me to sneak into the technology supply room and steal what I need to create lightning. I'll teleport to a remote island. Unlike some other beasts, I'm not a complete monster.

❤️ Liked by MILES2MILLAS and 11 others
GANKEd Saturday with my BOY!
MILES2MILLAS That 🍕 was for real the best idea we've ever had.

❤️ Liked by Jeff.Davis and RioM and 25 others
MILES2MILLAS #TBT was I or was I not the cutest baby you have ever seen in your life.
RioM ¡chévere! 😭 😭 😭

♥ Liked by Ayayron and Jeff.Davis and 27 others

MILES2MILLAS Name a more iconic duo. I'll wait.

Ayayron 😆

♥ Liked by RioM and 8 others

GANKEd what's @MILES2MILLAS playing?
Wrong answers only.

JJBROSEPH DUNGEONS AND DORKS???

GANKEd @JJBROSEPH Blocked

PRIVATE ENCRYPTED POST

Life in emoji right now: 😭🪦👽

Okay, but also, can we discuss the latest DLC of Elf vs Garbage Dump? Because I have no idea how to get past that part where you're playing as the teeny smol recyclable soda can and you have to somehow fight the evil Elf king, Vladisnot?

No, I am not distracting myself, why do you ask?

Fine. I asked E if he wanted to be on my team for this thing, and he hasn't answered. Who doesn't answer, like, right away?

SM, SG, and I are going to do some team building exercises tomorrow and I am . . . excited???

It's going to feel good having someone have my back. And it's going to feel good getting to back someone up!

CHAPTER 10

EXPLAIN IT AGAIN? I DON'T GET IT.

I SAID THAT OBVIOUSLY MS. MARVEL IS USING TIME TRAVEL DOWN TO HER ATOMS AND THAT'S HOW SHE GETS BIG AND SMALL! IT'S THE TINIEST PARTS THAT TRAVEL THROUGH TIME.

WHAT DOES THAT EVEN MEAN? SHE'S STILL THERE.

SESSION TERMINATED

KID IMMORTUS: Do you all seriously not understand it? It's as easy as +34%-27*

MAX FRANKENSTEIN: I don't think that math makes sense, but if you think it makes sense then who am I to spit on your dream.

KiD IMMORTUS: My plan, not my dream. You're not paying attention are you.

DEATH LOCKET: I literally have no idea what is going on.

KID APOCALYPSE: Same.

KID IMMORTUS: 😫

DEATH LOCKET: 🙁

KID APOCALYPSE: 🫠

KID IMMORTUS: FRANKENSTEIN COME BACK AND TELL ME WHY MY MATH IS WRONG. Is she not just in a constant state of time travel??!

DEATH LOCKET: Yeah, I don't think he's coming back. What if we just threw you into Latvia?

KID IMMORTUS: . . .

KID APOCALYPSE: What if you just stayed here and we can try to win the decathlon.

DEATH LOCKET: LOL

KID IMMORTUS: Why do I talk to any of you.

DEATH LOCKET: 👫

KID IMMORTUS: Look, Apocalypse, channel some of that energy from your namesake and get the job done okay?

Death Locket seems to think we're all friends. Is this friendship?

I think I have to say no to Ms. Marvel tomorrow, it feels like this is what I'm supposed to be doing. Kid Immortus had it right, I am who I am.

APOCALYPSE!

ME

Should I tell her that Kid Immortus has some weird plan for her, though? Would that be betraying my friends?

This is making my head hurt.

CHAPTER 11

CAPTAIN MARVEL: FOLLOW THE CHAIN OF COMMAND, BUT NEVER FORGET TO THINK FOR YOUSELF.

QUICKSILVER: PICK YOUR FAVORITE TEAMMATE. JUST KIDDING! (REALLY, THOUGH, REMEMBER THAT YOU'RE IN IT TOGETHER.)

SHE-HULK: THINK ABOUT WHAT YOU DO AND HOW IT WILL IMPACT YOUR TEAMMATES. IF YOU JUMP HIGH, IS THERE SOMEONE TO HANDLE THE LOWER GROUND?

CRYSTAL: STAND UP FOR WHAT'S RIGHT, EVEN IF IT MEANS GOING AGAINST THE STATUS QUO! TRUST YOUR INSTINCTS.

ANT-MAN: I'LL HANDLE THE LOWER GROUND! . . . SHE-HULK, I DON'T THINK THAT GROAN CAN BE COUNTED AS ADVICE.

FILE NAME: THE LAW AND YOU
PROFESSOR JENNIFER WALTERS, ESQUIRE

PROCEDURAL HISTORY: The class is a mixed group of students who use their real names publicly and those who need to wear a mask. Some have had trouble with the law before and some haven't.

ISSUE: How do we deal with the law? What about our secret identities? Some of us use them, and some don't. How do we navigate that?

A TRANSCRIPT OF OPENING REMARKS

JENNIFER WALTERS, ESQUIRE, AKA SHE-HULK: So, because I'm a practicing lawyer, I've been open about who I am and what I do. Also, who would cover this face up, am I right?

[Note: The students did not laugh.]

SHE-HULK: ANYway, I made that choice for myself and that's the right of every super hero here. You don't get to decide for someone else because you don't know who they might be protecting.

[Note: Ms. Marvel raises her hand.]

SHE-HULK: Yes, Ms. Marvel.

MS. MARVEL: So, this isn't related, strictly speaking, but—hypothetically speaking—you caused some very minor damage to some buildings in a populated area, no one got hurt! But, you know, some, uh, structural damage. Whose responsibility is it to clean it up? Sometimes I have, like, four seconds to do a fight and then I have to go to school or key club or something.

SPIDER-MAN: I'd also like to know this. I asked Spider-Man once but he just laughed and said, "Oh, you poor kid," and I don't know what that means.

AMERICA CHAVEZ: Yeah, I've been wondering about this, too.

BRAWN: Same.

NOVA: Yeah. But, like Ms. Marvel said, hypothetically.

SHE-HULK: That's a good question. You should always stick around and ask if people need help—

MS. MARVEL: Oh yeah, of course. But I mean the literal building and street cleaning.

SHE-HULK: And you're ALL wondering about this?

[Note: Every student in class raises their hand.]

SHE-HULK: How many buildings are you taking down???

Training was AWESOME. We're starting to gel as a team, and did you know?? That Miles can electrocute people? And Doreen can basically talk anyone into anything??

I was amazed. And being around each other now that we know who we all really are? Honestly? Incredible. It was so freeing.

We also started strategizing. That feels so grown-up. Strategizing. Miles reminded me that they listed out what the stages of the academic decathlon are—there are ten (duh) and they'll all use the stuff we've been learning at school.

We're definitely going to have to find our way through the Negative Zone I bet. I can feel it in my non-Adamantium bones.

(Sidenote: Wolverine has yet to be a guest lecturer at this school and I think that is completely bogus.)

(Sidenote x 2: Also Captain Marvel hasn't really been around too much? Mostly it's Vice Principal Maximoff running things. He's . . . interesting, but he's no Carol Danvers!)

Speaking of which, Miles and I were talking about the other Spider-Man (that's what Miles says!) and apparently there's going to be a Spider-People lecture?

- GUEST LECTURE -

YOU WANNA SWING LIKE SPIDER-PEOPLE?

THIS SATURDAY, 7PM
- TUESDAY AT 10AM

FREE PIZZA

(WHILE SUPPLIES LAST)

Me: Uh, how many Spider-People are there?

Miles: So many. It's awesome. But . . . really, so many.

Me: Wait, why does this say that the lecture is scheduled for two days?

Miles: A lot of Spider-People!!

126

127

School's Out for . . . EVIL

By: Slothbaby

CRRRASSSHHHH!!!!

Carol felt the metal crack open against her back. A huge humanoid cyborg had thrown her against the back of the wall of the training room. Air sucked out and into the open sky. She shook off the pain and hovered in the air, taking stressful seconds to survey the scene below her.

Director Fury had blown off the leg of the robot fighting him and was calling for backup. His voice sounded strained. He was hurt.

Monica! Where was Monica?!

She heard the familiar blip of a laser and saw her friend holding her own against not one, but two of these mechanical horrors.

And horrors they were! Some looked more human than others, but wrong. Gooey skin hung off their metal skeletons. But others just looked like they were straight out of that old space opera movie your dad made you watch over and over again. All angles and beat-up metal.

But they were strong.

She had to help.

She flung her bangs out of her eyes and flew down, fist first into the robot closest to her. A crunch of metal and she barely broke her momentum. Straight through what seemed like his head! She looked behind her and saw a bunch of metal pieces in her wake. Yes!!!

"Monica!!"

Her friend didn't pause firing, taking one robot through the eye and another through its tin can head.

"I've got this! Help the Director!!"

Carol glanced toward Fury, who was whispering into his communicator. She flew down to crouch next to him.

"I said you do not need to send her. I repeat, situation is under control. They're not ready."

"Director?" Carol didn't want to interrupt, but there was . . . uh, a lot going on. Fury looked at her and opened his mouth to answer, and neighed.

That couldn't be right.

No, the neighing was coming from above them. Carol looked up.

. . .

There was a horse. With wings. Flying above her head. Maybe she had hit her head earlier and didn't realize it? She looked back at Director Fury who was massaging his temples. The firing had stopped.

"Director Fury, is there a horse with wings up there, or am I having an episode of some kind?"

"Everything's good over here! I got the two robots—oh my god, Carol, there is a horse floating in the middle of the room."

Carol's eyes shot back up to the horse, this time looking at the rider.

"Val???!!!!!!"

A/N: HERE SHE COMES TO SAVE THE DAAAAAY. The team is now all together. But who sent the robots?? Who was Fury talking to??? Mwha ha ha, that's for me to know and you to find out.

COMMENTS

AcornLuvr   TO: Slothbaby, W3bbed4Life • 4 hours ago

YOU HAVE TO GIVE US SOME HINTS ABOUT WHAT HAPPENS OKAY JUST A FEW.

W3bbed4Life   TO: Evil, Slothbaby • 3 hours ago

Evil, Slothbaby, you are evil. How you gonna leave us hanging like that???

Slothbaby   TO: W3bbed4Life, AcornLuvr • 2 hours ago

What part of "Mwha ha ha" don't you guys understand?

Crzy4Cap   TO: Slothbaby • 1 hour ago

Hope Captain America shows up soon! But other than that, going great!

Evan's Journal KEEP OUT

Immortus has this idea about Ms. Marvel's powers and it doesn't make sense. But Max is going along with it because he is so busy with his experiment. And Death Locket's going along with it because she thinks that's how teams work. And I'm going along with it because I guess I'm . . . a bad person?

I don't feel like a bad person, I feel like a good person who is letting a bad thing happen. That kind of feels worse, actually.

Kid Immortus told me that all I have to do is convince Ms. Marvel to stand in a specific spot during the 10th task at the decathlon. It sounds so shady.

He was like, "Okay, Kid Apocalypse, you have a relationship with Ms. Marvel since you two have that class together. You'll get her to stand in this spot on the map and I'll use the anti-freeze ray that Frankenstein built to freeze her and force her to show me how to time travel."

I wish I'd said, "Nothing about that makes sense, Kid Immortus. I'm not doing it."

But I didn't. Instead I mumbled something and sat and watched Doctor Strange's weird crystal ball. Ugh.

Hm. Maybe there's a way I can let Ms. Marvel know this is happening?

CHAPTER 12

THE ACADEMIC DECATHLON LOOMS

The Institute Editorial Board

Students cry, "We're not ready!" as academic decathlon comes closer. "So get ready," responds Vice Principal Maximoff.

We are just a short ways out from Avengers Institute's very first academic decathlon. That's ten tasks every student team will have to complete in order to put into practice the training we've been subjected to—we mean, had the privilege to access—over the last few months.

So far Principal Danvers and Veep Maximoff have kept the actual trials strictly under wraps, but the staff at the *Avengers Institute Post* have managed to glance at a few wayward scraps of planning material found in the recycling bin outside of the vice principal's office.

Who is SL? What magic simulation can we expect?

There are, of course, rumors abound in the hallowed halls of the Institute.

"I heard that they're going to throw us to the bears," one student said.

"What bears?" another asked.

"You know, man, the bears." It must be noted that this editorial board found no evidence of bears. Write to us with any tips you might have! (You can also send an anonymous message if you'd like to keep your name out of this.)

NOTES ON INTERCEPTED PLANNING MATERIALS FOUND:

"Negative Zone??? Too dangerous???"

"Call Strange to create magic sim"

"Need cardboard"

"Email SL to say no"

So, I was hanging with Miles and Doreen and we were talking about the decathlon, because it's coming up (too) soon! But we started trying to guess what was going to happen and . . .

LOL

So at first Miles was like, "There'll probably be a redo of that rat alien room thing. I bet."

Of course, I had to say something as the leader. "Only this time, we'll be much better at working as a team!"

Doreen: Or we'll have to go to Atlantis and swim through Namor's throne room. Do they make tiny scuba gear for squirrels?

Me: What if it's just us, running through the Negative Zone in a double three-legged race?

Miles: Ha ha!! No wait, it's going to be us having to organize Professor Walters's case files in under 10 minutes.

Doreen: They're going to send us to the MOON!

And we'll have to see who can get the highest moon jump!

Me: To prove we can sneak, we are definitely going to have to steal from the King of Thieves himself, Gambit.

Anyway, I'm sure none of that is going to happen. But what are they going to throw at us?? I wonder if . . . I can email Captain Marvel? She did say she was always around (even though I've seen her, like, two times since starting at the Institute . . .).

A LIST OF BAD GUYS WE DO NOT WANT TO FIGHT*

*that are not the obvious, terrifying ones

Mole Man

- He's UNDERGROUND, he's mean, and he's using the name of a rodent without caring about them.

The Spot

- What if he puts you into an infinite loop of falling dark holes, just top to the bottom, over and over again forever.

SCREWBALL

- Ugh, Screwball is so annoying. Like, you never know when she'll just use you to go viral.

VENOM

- I thought were weren't adding the obvious, terrifying ones.

- This one couldn't hurt to repeat, I mean. Really. I don't want to fight Venom. I bet it's so hard to get that drool out of your costume.

The Owl

- Did You Know that Owls eat squirrels????

M.O.D.O.K.

BLAH, BLAH
AH

- I heard M.O.D.O.K. just never stops talking. Always yapping. No, thanks!

THE OTHER SPIDER-MAN: How's it going, kid? You ready for this heca-deca-octo-athalon?

MILES: Ermmm mostly. What do you hear about it?

THE OTHER SPIDER-MAN: Ha ha! Nice try. Carol would kick my b-u-t-t if I told you what to expect.

MILES: Ugh fine! Any advice?

THE OTHER SPIDER-MAN: Stay strong.

MILES: This is the opposite of helpful.

THE OTHER SPIDER-MAN: Okay, look I heard there was a hamster wheel.

MILES: WHAT!

TRAINING REGIMEN for Squirrel Girl and Tippy-Toe

BY Doreen Green

Squirrel Girl:
- 200 push-ups
- 200 chin-ups overhanded
- 15 laps around Central Park
- Five square meals a day
- 200 squats
- 200 tail swings
- 200 tail lifts

Tippy-Toe
- 5 push-ups
- 5 chin-ups underhanded
- 5 acorns a day
- 15 frolicks in the meadow
- 20 tail swings
- 20 tail lifts

TO: Carol Danvers <cdanvers@avengers-institute.com>

FROM: Kamala Khan <k-khan2014@heatmail.com>

Subject: Quick meeting?

Principal Danvers,

I was wondering if I could meet with you for a few minutes sometime this week? I have some questions about the academic decathlon.

Thank you so much.

Kamala

TO: Kamala Khan <k-khan2014@heatmail.com>

FROM: Carol Danvers <cdanvers@avengers-institute.com>

Subject: AUTOMATIC REPLY RE: Quick meeting?

Apologies. I'm out of the office due to an intergalactic invasion of Earth. If this is urgent, please email Vice Principal Maximoff (pmaximoff@ avengers-institute.com). Otherwise, I will reply on my return next week.

Best,

Col. Carol Danvers

Principal, Avengers Institute

CHAPTER 13

AVENGERS INSTITUTE

DEAR STUDENT:

Today's the day! We're excited to kick off the first ever Avengers Institute Academic Decathlon. Some things to keep in mind:

• As the name implies, there will be ten trials.

• You will have fifteen minutes to finish each trial, after which you must begin the next trial.

• The trials will begin promptly. If you're late, you will not have any time added in order to finish.

• If you find yourself in a situation where you're stuck, please remember that you can use your communicators to hail a teacher and someone will come get you.

• You are not only being graded on your ability to finish the trials efficiently, but also how well you implement what you've learned this semester.

• There is a translating mode on your communicator should you need it.

• There is a zero-tolerance policy for harming your competitors.

Oh my god oh my god oh my god oh my god oh my god it's the day today's the day we are not ready but we can do this I think.

It turns out Principal (Captain? Colonel?) Danvers wasn't around to talk. But she'll be here today for the decathlon. She's the principal. This was probably her idea! I just wish we knew what to expect.

Miles said he heard through the grapevine, whatever that means, that there's a hamster wheel or something?

Miles, Doreen, and I have been training nonstop, though. Our teamwork's never been better! We've got this. We've totally got this.

Do I sound like I'm trying to convince myself?

Deep breaths, deep breaths, deep breaths.

I talked to Abu about getting ready for this. Obviously no specifics, but he quoted this verse from the Quran that says, "Indeed with hardship is ease." Which sounds confusing, but then he explained: There's relief in working hard.

We've worked so hard to get here, and the decathlon's going to be hard, but it's going to feel good when we're doing it, and that I can look forward to.

AVENGERS INSTITUTE ACADEMIC DECATHLON
TRIAL ONE
"WHO ARE YOU?"
Interviews conducted by Jennifer Walters, Esquire

SUBJECT: Nova (17 of 45)

PROFESSOR JENNIFER WALTERS, ESQUIRE: I said, WHO ARE YOU?
NOVA: My name is Nova, ma'am! I have no other name, ma'am!
WALTERS: If you don't tell me your name, I'm going to blow up the
moon.
NOVA: What? Can you do that? Who are you in this scenario? Are you
strong enough to PUNCH THE MOON AND EXPLODE IT?
WALTERS: Ugh, never mind. You're through.
NOVA: AW YES.
WALTERS: Send the next one in. [Note: Ms. Walters let out a deep sigh.]

SUBJECT: Ms. Marvel (39 of 45)

WALTERS: Okay, Ms. Marvel. You tell me your real identity right now
or I'll—
MS. MARVEL: I don't think so!
[Note: Sounds of crashing and smashing. Goes on for several minutes.
Finally the cacophony simmers to a small rattle.]
WALTERS: Ms. Marvel! You embiggened in the classroom.
MS. MARVEL: AND I tied you up! No leverage!
WALTERS: . . . You're technically right. Go on.

SUBJECT: Spider-Man (45 of 45)

WALTERS: Spider-Man! Tell me your name!
SPIDER-MAN: What if I don't.
WALTERS: You know what, yes. You pass. I swear, I told Pietro that this
wouldn't work.
SPIDER-MAN: Ermmmm.
WALTERS: Said all I had to do was ask, they'd crack. Didn't listen, but
no, he's vice principal, and . . .
[Note: Ms. Walters's voice fades out.]
SPIDER-MAN: I guess . . . I win?

CAPTAIN MARVEL: Scott! I did not approve students getting shrunk! You said you were doing a treasure hunt!

ANT-MAN: It is a treasure hunt! It's just a very small treasure. Anyway, they're doing great! Ms. Marvel's team is seconds away from getting to the exit, and I'm pretty sure Kid Immortus just had Death Locket blast through one of the cardboard walls to get to the end, so we are A-okay. Also, I did leave a note on Pietro's desk . . .

CAPTAIN MARVEL: . . . Did you even test the shrinking ray or whatever it is you used?

ANT-MAN: Of course!

CAPTAIN MARVEL: On something carbon-based???

ANT-MAN: I might have shrunk the note . . .

CAPTAIN MARVEL: Scott.

TRIAL TEN:
THIRTY MINUTES AROUND THE WORLDS

In each location, each team will be asked to pick up a piece of an artifact. There is a piece for every team. Once you find your specific artifact, then a portal will open to the next level. Only when each team has all six pieces will they be able to reenter the school.

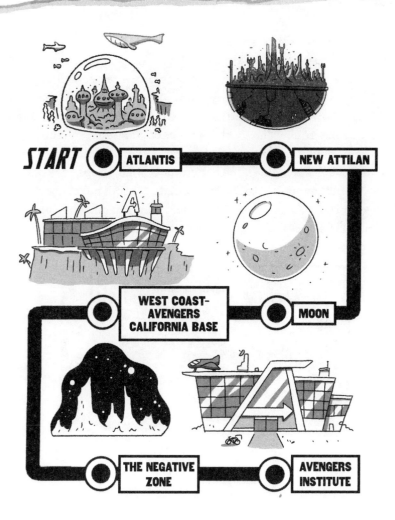

START ● ATLANTIS

● NEW ATTILAN

● WEST COAST-AVENGERS CALIFORNIA BASE

● MOON

● THE NEGATIVE ZONE

● AVENGERS INSTITUTE

CHAPTER 14

IT'S TIME FOR THE TENTH TRIAL LIVEBLOG

Brought to you by your intrepid editorial staff here at the *Institute Post*. We get to the places you don't want to go!

:30 seconds—Okay, so first thing's first, the teams have to get to Atlantis. Now, we are watching on the same cameras that the professors are judging, so we'll see everything they see. It looks like Team Ms. Marvel, Spider-Man, and Squirrel Girl are in the lead! It's been less than thirty seconds and these kids already have their eyes on the first artifact piece! Ms. Marvel stretches her arm out and loops it around the little jagged piece of ceramic, zipping around fish and various Atlanteans to get her hands on it! This seems like it's going to be a piece of cake for our Avengers Institute friends!

1:07—Uh-oh, we spoke too soon. It looks like Namorita was hiding in the, er, waves to shake things up! Ms. Marvel and her team got through, but Nova, America, and the Wasp are in some trouble. Can they get through Namorita's defenses?

1:23—They CAN! As can all our teams! Though it looked like Kid Apocalypse almost didn't get through the portal to make it to New Attilan. Good thing his energy blasts could push him through the water like that. His team didn't seem to notice, and that is definitely going to cost them some points.

1:42—Yikes, New Attilan seems to be a stumper for everyone. It's been at least fifteen seconds since they all made it through, but no one's found their artifact piece yet. Professors Lockjaw and Crystal are on the ground, not giving anything away, but definitely taking notes.

1:54—Twelve more precious seconds gone and finally some action. A giant black beetle has crawled out of a wall to waylay the teams and it is working! Doesn't look like anyone's noticed the artifact pieces sitting on top of the beetle's back—oh! Spidey swings from above and grabs a piece while Ms. Marvel and Squirrel Girl throw him matching thumbs-ups! Who could have seen that coming!

2:08—It was quick work once Spidey cracked the code, and all our teams have found their artifacts and made it through to THE MOON. Where were they keeping those space helmets? Anyway, let's not think too hard about how much magic is at work during this decathlon or it will make our heads hurt.

2:15—Okay, the Watcher is just . . . watching. Creepy but in line with the job description. It looks like America Chavez is getting ready to punch some moon rock out of the way, and won't that be exciting in the gravity they're in!

2:22—SQUIRREL GIRL JUST SHAKES EVERYTHING UP, pulling their artifact piece out of a glowing box, buried in the moon dust. The Marvel-Spidey-Squirrel team is killing it out there, today. They are working like a well-oiled machine. You love to see it!

2:30—Not everyone's having as easy a time, it looks like Kid Immortus is too busy sneaking up on the Marvel team to help his own out too much. Why is he so close on Ms. Marvel's heels when all his other teammates are so far behind? And . . . oh! Max Frankenstein has been holding on to their artifact piece without letting the rest of his team know! Ooh, we would not want to be on the other end of a Beast lecture, that is for sure.

SNAPSHOTS FROM THE INSTITUTE:

Vice Principal Maximoff says "NO!" to flavored water in the vending machines.

Professor Lang seen shrinking down outside Professor McCoy's classroom. What's that about?

Evan's Journal KEEP OUT

So, I listened to Kid Immortus. Because I'm awful. I followed Ms. Marvel, Spider-Man, and Squirrel Girl because I thought that's what teammates did.

They were pretty far ahead of me so by the time I caught up we were almost at the castle.

"Hey, Ms. Marvel!"

And of course, because she's a nice person she turned around immediately, and then again, immediately asked if I—the guy who was about to help his teammate capture her for reasons that most of us did not understand—needed help.

"Evan! Hey! Where's your team, oh man, do you need help? Spidey! Squirrel Girl, hold up! We've gotta help Evan!"

And her teammates, because they are also good people, put the decathlon on hold and stopped to listen to me in case something was wrong.

"No, uh, I just wanted to check in—how's the trial going?"

I can't blame them for all looking at me like I was losing it.

"Well, we're still missing our last piece, but really . . . Dude, where's your team?" Spider-Man was not interested in my terrible stalling tactics.

"They're uh . . . I mean . . . They're around here somewhere? I just saw you and wanted to say hi."

"Evan, what is going on? You're being really weird."

"Is this what he's usually like, Ms. Marvel?" If only you knew, Squirrel Girl! I almost walked right then. Just left. But right as I was about to . . . the rest of my team showed up.

It didn't go well.

"THANKS, KID APOCALYPSE! We're here to take Ms. Marvel, and you should just stand aside, Spider-Dork and whoever you are." Kid Immortus sometimes tries a little hard to be villainous and it's embarrassing to see. I know he knows who Squirrel Girl is!

"Excuse you? Spider-WHAT NOW"

"We have two classes together, Kid Immortus. You know my name. Don't be a jerk!"

"Seriously, what is going on?"

And then I broke. What was I doing???

"Ms. Marvel! I'm sorry, Kid Immortus wants to—well, I'm not sure what exactly. He has some weird plan, and it involves you, and I thought I was supposed to help them because I'm evil, but you're my friend and I don't want you to get hurt!"

"KID APOCALYPSE! What are you doing?! I need her atoms!!!" That was the end of my first team. (Or maybe) . . .

And then Ms. Marvel proved why she's awesome. Out of all that I just said, out of me telling her I betrayed her, that it's my fault, she says:

"Evan! You're not evil!"

Hands Off!

Okay, so, let me clue you in on what went on during our final trial. Evan showed up, acted like a complete rando, and then Kid Immortus, Death Locket, and Max Frankenstein tried to kidnap me.

I don't even know.

Well, okay, mostly it was Kid Immortus and Death Locket. Max kept being like, "You've tried it, old chap, and it didn't work, let's truck on!"

(Or something, I guess he's more 1800s talk than . . . a bad Sherlock Holmes adaptation, but you get the point.)

Anyway, Evan tells me what's going on. Miles totally jumps up to clock Kid Immortus! My hero??? Even though he didn't have to and I could have done it. I was a little shell-shocked from being randomly targeted and the center of a whole super villain plot without even realizing it. Usually with these things (RIP: normal use of the word "usually") I know what's going on, I know who I'm fighting, I know that I'm in a fight! But this was out of nowhere. Luckily, I had my friends there to help me out. If I'd tried to do that on my own? I don't even want to think about it.

So, I have to start shouting, too, because how else am I going to be heard. (Hello, have you ever been to an aunties-and-uncles party and everyone is so loud and the loudest person wins? I win.) I yell: "YOU CAN'T HAVE MY ATOMS!"

Granted, I probably should have come up with something better, like, "No atoms on the menu today, but how about a knuckle sandwich." Or, "I'm ATOMICALLY displeased!"

But I didn't, I just yelled the first thing I thought of and then I wrapped Kid Immortus in my giant fist, and threw him across the Negative Zone and it felt really good.

We tried asking Death Locket and Max Frankenstein what exactly Kid Immortus was trying to do, and they could not answer us. I ask you, what kind of team????

They did show me some weird equation he tried to sell them on, but it looks like they were just kind of going along with it to go along with it.

And that's why you shouldn't listen to charismatic leaders who aren't actually saying anything. Evan's explanation was my favorite, though.

Evan really thought he was evil. Because his team made him think he belonged there, and that's awful. I look back at how afraid I was to go to this school and trust my teammates, and I'm so glad I have people in my life who can help me through these decisions. Evan doesn't have that! So, I'm going to try and be ~~that friend~~ for him.

Unfortunately, because of Kid Immortus trying to steal my atoms and generally maybe destroy me? We lost. Even though we were in the lead. Which sucks, but I am alive, so priorities?

NOVA, AMERICA, WASP: FIRST PLACE

Of COURSE, how could I even be mad.
They're all so awesome!!

AMADEUS CHO, PATRIOT, IRONHEART: SECOND PLACE

They came back big from that rat-alien disaster, good for
them!

MOON GIRL & DEVIL DINOSAUR: THIRD PLACE

Poor Moon Girl, Devil Dinosaur was never going to make it past the illusion of
paella on the California beach.

MS. MARVEL, SPIDER-MAN, SQUIRREL GIRL: FOURTH PLACE

We're pretty awesome, too! Considering we would've won
if it hadn't been for the evildoers!

**KID IMMORTUS, KID APOCALYPSE, MAX FRANKENSTEIN, DEATH
LOCKET:** DISQUALIFIED

Note to self: Reach out to Evan and make sure he's okay!

CHAPTER 15

Chapter 5

School's Out for . . . EVIL

By: Slothbaby

"Val??!!!"

"Carol?!?!"

"Um."

"EVERYONE, QUIET. PLEASE LINE UP AND STAND IN FRONT OF ME."

Director Fury shouted that last bit. Carol was stunned. What was her friend Val doing on a flying horse—a pegasus—at her training session?

"Carol, this is Valkyrie of the Asgardians."

Carol whipped her head around and stared at the friend she thought she knew.

"Excuse me?!"

"Ms. Danvers, do I need to remind you that you are still in training on board my ship and that we just almost had our butts handed to us by a bunch of robots? Now is not the time."

"Yes, sir."

"And Ms.—" Fury hesitated for the slightest second, showing Carol that he wasn't as okay as he was pretending to be. "Valkyrie. Thank you for coming, but as you can see, we have handled the threat."

"Wait, um, sir, could I just have a minute to talk to Valkyrie?" Carol could feel Monica's eyes on her, questioning. But she had to know what her friend from school was doing here.

"You're lucky I need to do a quick mission report, Danvers. At ease."

Carol wasted no time.

"Val! What the heck!"

Val was laughing, hopping off her horse.

"I could ask you the same thing!"

"What are you doing here? Asgardian?? What is going on??"

"I'm a trainee, just like you, I guess! But they made me go undercover since I'm technically doing a foreign exchange program."

Monica interrupted then, shoving out a hand. "Hi! I'm Monica Rambeau. Pilot and best friend to this one."

"Nice to meet you, Monica. I go to school with Carol, but, uh, no one told us that we were both in this program."

"I have to admit, Val, my head's spinning." She ran a hand through her short blond hair.

"I know, I know! I wanted to tell you!" Val frowned. "But I wasn't allowed. They said they'd send me back."

BRUNO: . . . He wanted to time travel using . . . atoms?

KAMALA: ¯_(ツ)_/¯

BRUNO: It's not making you think about your actual atoms, like what's in them?

KAMALA: Positive there's a proton and it's not negative that there's an electron lol

BRUNO: What about the kids who tried to take UR ATOMS

KAMALA: I'm meeting w Captain Marvel tmrw and gonna talk to her about it. And Evan said his team is gonna be assigned 2 intense independent study or something. Hopefully, they'll get better.

BRUNO: That's good tho! Cap will *def* be helpful, she'll understand better than most.

CAPTAIN MARVEL AND MS. MARVEL: A conversation

SETTING: Captain Marvel's principal's office. There's a big desk. CAROL is seated behind it, an open laptop to her left. KAMALA sits in a chair in front of her.

CAPTAIN MARVEL: Hello, Kamala, I called you in because I saw your email just a day too late to talk to you before the decathlon. But I wanted to be sure that we met.

KAMALA: Ah yeah, yes, no worries, I mean, you didn't apologize, but I'm just saying it's fine. I know you're probably busy.

CAPTAIN MARVEL: [rubs at her temples] Yes and no. When I started at this school, it was as a part-time professor. I don't think I realized the workload and the amount of meetings being principal involved or—top secret—I would have made Pietro do it.

KAMALA: [laughs] Vice Principal Maximoff would have hated that.

CAPTAIN MARVEL: He would have, and I think maybe our decathlon wouldn't have run as smoothly as it did—although it didn't run that smoothly for you, did it?

KAMALA: I was surprised by how well it did go at first! But, I did want to ask: Do you have any advice on how to deal with the idea of someone trying to hurt me without me even knowing about it?

CAPTAIN MARVEL: I hate to say it, but it's part of the nature of our jobs. But the first thing is knowing that you don't have to do this on your own, and that you have friends to help. It sounds like Spider-Man and Squirrel Girl and even Evan were there for you.

KAMALA: They were! And Evan, oh man. What's going to happen to his team? Kid Immortus and the rest?

CAPTAIN MARVEL: Oh, we're assigning each of them to a traveling teacher. It was too soon to put them in with a large group of students. I think Kid Immortus is working with Bishop, Death Locket's with Vision, and Max Frankenstein is with Mr. Fantastic. I do need to apologize to you, though. We should have caught on earlier. I've noted that we should bring on another teacher next semester, to help keep an eye on things.

KAMALA: Thank you—but even with all that . . . whatever, I have to say, Captain, that this was the best. I feel like I learned so much!

CAPTAIN MARVEL: I'm glad! I know it didn't necessarily seem like it, but the professors have kept me informed about all the kids and their progress over the last few months. You're a strong student, and it's great that you've built a strong team, Kamala. This is exactly what we hoped for when we started the Institute. I'm so proud of you.

KAMALA: [sitting up straight in her chair, grinning widely, holding out her cell phone] . . . Could you say that one more time, just into this voice memo here. I'd, uh, really like to play it for the rest of the team.

CAPTAIN MARVEL: [laughing] I guess you've earned that much. [leans into phone] I said YOUR TEAM DID WELL, AND I'M PROUD OF YOU.

Name: Ms. Marvel

Most proud of: My team!!

One thing you learned: Okay, this is going to sound so sentimental but . . . I learned that being a hero in my own way doesn't mean being a hero on my own. And that you never stop growing, and that you never stop learning from the amazing people around you. Shout-out to Spidey, Squirrel Girl, and my boy Evan!!

Name: Spider-Man

Most proud of: Ms. Marvel said she's gonna say our team, so I'm gonna cheat and say my friends!

One thing you learned: Squirrel Girl taught me how to bullet journal and it changed my life, and I am the most organized. Who knew that writing things down helped so much???

Name: Squirrel Girl

Most proud of: Ummm, I'm going to say the fact that we made it through the decathlon! Like, that was a TOUGH nut and we cracked it! We're the best! Team Stretchy Animals! (Is a spider an animal?)

One thing you learned: That I can make a difference!

Name: Evan Sabahnur

Most proud of: . . . Myself? I learned that just because other people put me in a box, it doesn't mean I have to stay in that box. I can be whoever I want to be! (Also oblig: Proud of my FRIENDS! I have friends!!)

One thing you learned: That I don't have to bend to peer pressure.

EVAN: We can hang out during the break, right?

MS. MARVEL: Yes! I need my super-hangs!

SPIDER-MAN: Yeah, as long as it doesn't take away from M's writing time. I have got 2 find out wat happens 2 Val & Carol.

EVAN: ???

SQUIRREL GIRL: www.EmbiggenFeels.moomblr.com/storyid=23942304/School's-Out-For-Evil

MS. MARVEL: !!!!!!!

SPIDER-MAN: We def lost Evan till he's done reading lol

MS. MARVEL: I'm so embarrassed omg

SQUIRREL GIRL: What friends are 4!!

Welcome, MS. MARVEL.

END OF SEMESTER REPORT CARD

INTRODUCTION TO BEING A HERO—PASS
Notes from Dr. Henry McCoy
Ms. Marvel was a joy to have in class! Highly
capable, adaptable, and her confidence grew every
week. Very impressed with her leadership abilities.

RIGHTS AND WRONGS AND IN BETWEEN—PASS
Notes from Professor Jennifer Walters, Esquire
Ms. Marvel handled herself well both in the
decathlon and during my class. She sometimes went
off-topic, but it was frequently due to her passion
and dedication to learning the truth. I respect
that.

INTERDIMENSIONAL TRAVEL & DIPLOMACY—PASS
Notes from Professor Crystal
I have nothing but wonderful things to say about
Ms. Marvel, a fellow Inhuman! Though a little timid
in the beginning, she was leading the charge by the
end. She was also a very engaged student, and truly
listened. An important skill to have in the super
hero world.

INDEPENDENT STUDY—PASS

I cannot believe this is all over!!

I cannot believe I made friends.

. . . I hung out with Bruno and Nakia earlier since I have an Institute break and maybe we all had a lot of sugar and now I am AMPED!!!!

Okay, really, though. Who knew that I'd make new best friends, I'd figure out how to be a better hero and believe in myself, and I'd get to sit down and hang out with Captain Marvel.

Past-me never would have believed it, so I guess maybe past-me is who started this journal entry, huh. I've been back on the job in Jersey City for a week now, and I am happy to report that not a single building has fallen down—but that even if one did, I know how to handle it now (thanks, Professor Walters!).

And I haven't been overwhelmed, but if I am, I know I can call for backup (thanks, Professor McCoy!).

Spidey, Squirrel Girl, Evan, and I have already hung out, and Spidey took us patrolling in his neighborhood. It was fun!

Next week, we're going to go to Squirrel Girl's. Ahhh! I have super friends!

I guess I can't wait to see where we go next!

PREETI CHHIBBER has written for SYFY, BookRiot, BookRiot Comics, The Nerds of Color, and The Mary Sue. She has work in the anthology A *Thousand Beginnings and Endings*, a collection of retellings of fairy tales and myths, and is the author of the *Spider-Man: Far from Home* tie-in *Peter and Ned's Ultimate Travel Journal* for Marvel. She hosts the podcasts Desi Geek Girls and Strong Female Characters (SYFYWire) and has appeared on several panels at New York Comic Con, San Diego Comic Con, and on screen on the SYFY Network.

JAMES LANCETT is a London-based illustrator, director and yellow sock lover! As a child growing up in Cardiff, he was obsessed with cartoons, video games and all things fantasy. As he grew up and became a lot more beardy these inspirations held strong and so he moved to London to study BA Illustration and Animation at Kingston University. This degree opened the door to a job he had dreamt of ever since he was a kid and he now works as an illustrator and animation director.